HARRIET and the ROLLER COASTER

HARRIET and the ROLLER COASTER

Nancy Carlson

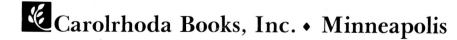Carolrhoda Books, Inc. ◆ Minneapolis

Manufactured in the United States of America

LIBRARY OF CONGRESS CATALOGING IN PUBLICATION DATA

Carlson, Nancy L.
   Harriet and the roller coaster.

   Summary: Harriet accepts her friend George's
challenge to ride the frightening roller
coaster, and finds out that she is the brave
one.
   [1. Dogs—Fiction. 2. Rabbits—Fiction.
3. Courage—Fiction. 4. Amusement rides—
Fiction] I. Title.
PZ7.C21665Hap   [E]   81-18138
ISBN 0-87614-183-1   AACR2

         4   5   6   7   8   9   10   92   91   90   89   88

for Jeanne and Mary,
because they take the chances I don't!

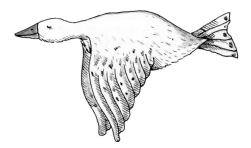

On the last day of school, Harriet's whole
class was going to the amusement park.
Everyone looked forward to the day.

"I bet you're too scared to ride the roller coaster. You'd probably start crying."

"I am *not* scared," said Harriet. "I'll ride on your old roller coaster. You just wait and see."

"I'm going to ride on the big roller coaster,"
George told Harriet. "It's so big, you can't
see the top. I know. My big sister told me."

"It goes so fast that if you don't hold on you'll fall right out."

That night Harriet didn't sleep very well.

The next morning, when it was time to get on the bus for the amusement park, she felt a little sick.

"See you on the roller coaster," said George. "If you don't chicken out."

As soon as they got to the amusement park,
George said, "Come on, Harriet. Let's get
our tickets for the roller coaster. Unless
you're too scared."

"I am *not* scared," said Harriet.

"Good," said George. "Then hurry up."

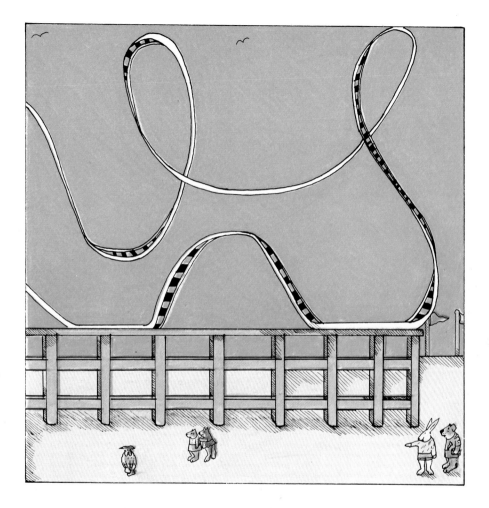

"Oh, boy," said George.

"I can't wait!"

"We're next. . . .

There's still time for you to chicken out."

"Here we go. Harriet, you're going to be sooooo scared."

The roller coaster went up and up. Harriet
had never been so high.

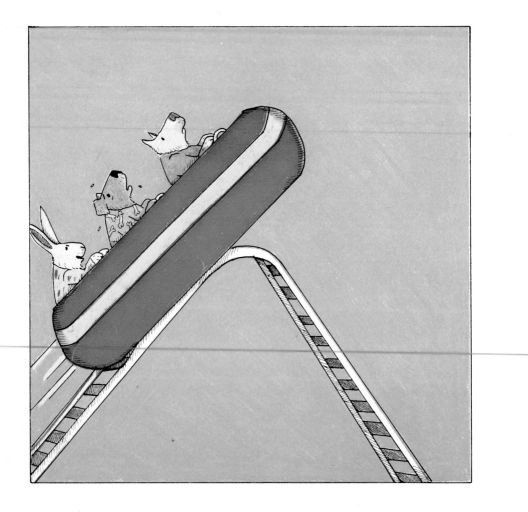

"This is great," said George.

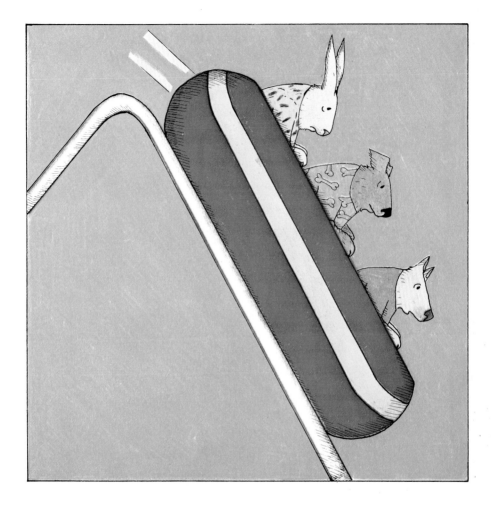

Then they were over the top.

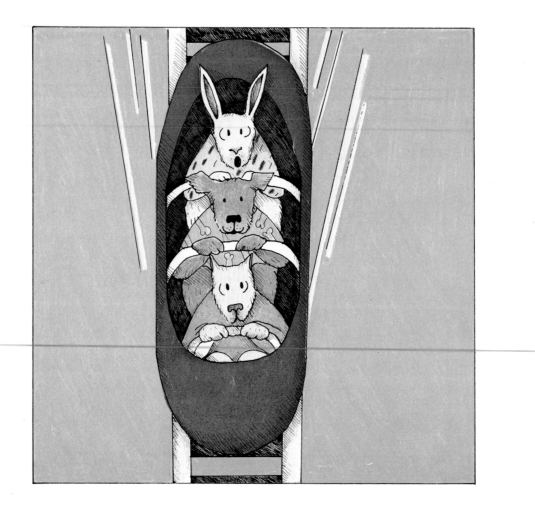

"Hey!" said Harriet. "This isn't so bad."
"Ooof!" said George.

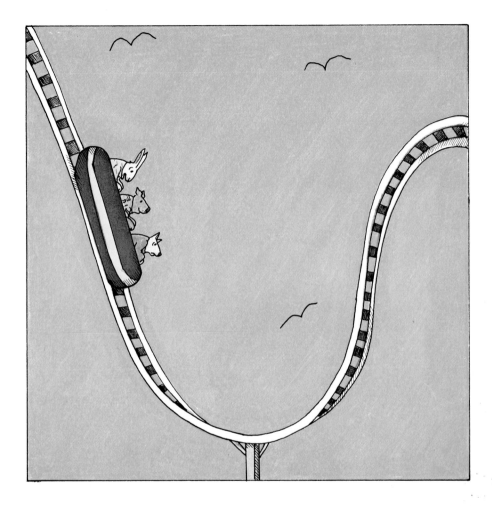

"I like it!" said Harriet.
"Help!" said George.

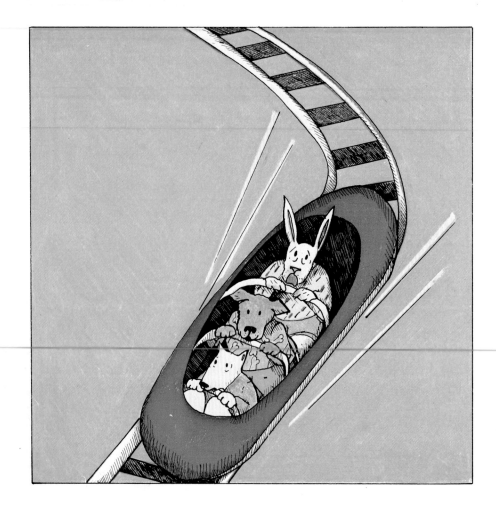

"Yippee!" yelled Harriet.
"Mommy!" yelled George.

"Is it over already?" said Harriet.

"I'm going again. That was fun!"
"I'd better sit down," said George.

So Harriet rode the roller coaster all day
long . . .

... while George sat quietly on a bench.